CHRISTMAS MYSTERIES

A Collection of Christmas Crime and Mystery Stories

CHRISTMAS MYSTERIES

David Dell

Happy Christmas!

David Dell

ALSO BY DAVID DELL

Crime Novels
THIRTEEN
THE BRIDE WORE BLACK

Short Stories
TALES FROM THE SHED

CHRISTMAS MYSTERIES

Contents

THE CHRISTMAS ANGEL

The year had started disastrously for Gordon. He had been helping his wife take down the Christmas decorations when the cat playfully pulled a string of fairy lights around the rungs of his stepladder.

Luckily, the cat wasn't hurt. But Gordon was off work for six weeks, with his leg in plaster. When he finally returned to the office, his desk had gone. The secretary scuttled in with a message that the boss wanted to see him.

Redundant at fifty-three. He'd received a reasonable pay-off, but it didn't begin to compensate for the blow to his self-esteem. And of course, finding another management position at his age would be pretty well impossible.

It was December before he started working again, at Jacksons, the department store. The job was only temporary and the pay was pathetic, but he had his own little office, if you could call it that. They also supplied a uniform. A red coat trimmed with white fur. And of course, a long white beard and black wellies.

He really hadn't wanted this job. At the interview, he'd been deliberately grumpy and told them he couldn't stand children. The Personnel Manager had given him an odd smile and told him to start the next day. Gordon hated that Personnel Manager. Lance Littlejohn, his name was. They'd been at school together all those years ago.

Somehow, Gordon coped with being pleasant to the children each day, but he was thankful when Christmas Eve arrived. His final day as Santa.

He'd written a letter for Lance Littlejohn. He read it through once more.

'Dear Littlebrain (as we used to call you),

You haven't changed a bit since schooldays. You're still despicable. I daresay you've completely forgotten that day in the school canteen when you threw a Brussels sprout at the Head. Sitting there, looking so innocent. He blamed me and I got the cane, but I still didn't tell on you. I wish I had now.

I can't forgive your smug look when you gave me this Santa Claus job. You must think it's the sort of menial work I'm cut out for. Well, thank heavens it ends today. It'll be a pleasure to go back to the Job Centre!'

Gordon wrote his name clearly at the bottom and sealed the letter in an envelope. He went into work early and left the letter on Lance Littlejohn's desk.

His last day in the grotto passed quickly. At twenty-past five there was just one little girl left to see him. His final customer. 'Come in, child,' he called.

'Hello, Santa,' said a sultry voice from the doorway.

Gordon looked up. 'I'm sorry,' he said, 'I thought you were a little girl.'

She gave a wicked smile. She was wearing a skimpy, low-cut dress, held up by two tiny straps. 'Do I look like a little girl?' she asked. 'I'm Angela. I'm a Christmas Angel.'

He gulped. 'Are you now? W...well, I'm sorry, but I'm afraid you're too old to receive one of Santa's gifts.'

'That's okay,' said Angela. 'I've come to see if there's anything *you'd* like for Christmas. Can I sit down?'

'Oh, er, of course,' said Gordon, pointing to the chair next to his.

Angela ignored the chair and lowered herself onto his lap, wrapping an arm round his shoulder. 'It's years since I sat on Santa's knee,' she said.

He swallowed hard, unsure whether to pull his face away from her cleavage.

'So, what would you like?' she purred. 'Let's see if I can grant your wish.'

'Who are you?'

'You don't recognise me in my party dress, do you? I'm Angela, Lance Littlejohn's secretary. We've been having an office party.'

'Have you been drinking, Angela?'

'Of course! I'm not normally like this. Come on, loosen up. It's Christmas!'

'I don't feel Christmassy.'

'Tell Angela all about it.'

Gordon took a deep breath. 'I haven't got a job,' he said.

Angela burst out laughing. 'Well, you can always help me. Lance often makes me work late.'

'I bet he does,' mumbled Gordon. 'Come on, you'd best be off now. Happy Christmas to you, Angela.'

She smiled. 'I've brought you a Christmas card,' she said, slipping it into his pocket. 'From your Christmas angel. It'll bring you luck.' She kissed him on the forehead and was gone.

Gordon felt odd. Then an unwelcome face appeared around the door. Lance Littlejohn.

'Ah, Gordon, old chap. Can you report back for duty on 2 January?'

'Oh, ha ha. I don't think there'll be much call for Santa Claus in January, do you?'

'Of course not. But the Managing Director needs a Personal Assistant.'

Gordon stared at him. 'Are you serious?'

'Of course. It's a very responsible job and extremely well paid. You'll be perfect. I knew as soon as I saw your CV.'

'So why did you take me on as Santa?'

'The MD wanted me to recruit his assistant from somebody already on the staff. So, I employed you as Santa first to get over the problem.'

'I don't know what to say.'

'Don't say anything. I'm repaying a favour, something that goes back to our schooldays. You won't remember. It was all about a Brussels sprout. Anyway, must dash. I've had a really busy day. I haven't even had a chance to look at this morning's post yet. Happy Christmas, Gordon!'

The awful significance of Lance's last words hit Gordon like a smack on the chin. He buried his head in his hands. 'Why did I have to write that stupid letter?'

14

Despondently, he took off his red coat, and then noticed Angela's Christmas card sticking out of the pocket. Only it wasn't a Christmas card.

Gordon chuckled. She really was a Christmas angel. He looked down again at the writing on the envelope.

It was his letter to Lance Littlejohn.

- *First Published in* Bella *Magazine*

CHRISTMAS PRESENCE

The two boys tramped through the snow, following the lamplighter on his rounds through Camden Town until they reached Charlie's house, a two-storey brick-built property with a row of iron railings outside.

Charlie turned to his friend. 'You look frozen, Timothy. Let's go indoors. We'll ask my mother for some hot lemon cordial.'

The smaller boy's eyes widened. 'Do you think she'd give us some?'

'Of course she will. Come on.'

As they opened the front door, Charlie's mother called out. 'Don't come in for a moment.'

'It's cold out here.'

'Come in then, but keep your eyes closed tightly until I tell you to open them.'

Charlie gave his friend an indulgent smile and they both closed their eyes.

'I won't be a moment boys, I'm just making a few final adjustments.'

'Can we look yet?' Charlie asked.

'Another few seconds,' she said. 'And...we're ready.'

They opened their eyes and stared. Little Timothy looked fascinated. 'A tree? You've brought a tree indoors?'

Before them, in an earthenware pot, was a fir tree, about five feet high. Here and there amongst the branches hung hook-ended sugar canes. Clipped to some of the boughs were small lighted candles, giving the room a warm glow. At the very top of the tree was fixed a tinsel star.

Charlie grinned. 'It's a *Christmas* tree. Everyone has them in Germany. I read about it in father's newspaper.'

His mother raised her eyes. 'Since when did a ten-year-old read *The Times*? Anyway, do you like the tree?'

'It's brilliant,' Charlie said.

Timothy was gently touching one of the branches. He moved closer and sniffed the pine needles.

'Are you all right?' Charlie asked.

Tears were dribbling down Timothy's cheeks. 'I wish we could have a Christmas tree at *our* house.'

'We could go across the fields to Morgan's meadow. There are trees there. We could cut one down for you.'

'Farmer Morgan might not be amused,' said Charlie's mother.

Timothy had recovered now. 'We haven't room in our house, anyway. There are nine of us and our living room is tiny. But it's lovely seeing your tree. And I love those sugar canes.'

19

'Call over on Christmas morning and you shall have one. If your parents allow you out, of course. They may like you to stay at home with them over the holiday.'

'They won't mind me going out. Father's working, anyway.'

'On Christmas Day? He must have an important position.'

Timothy considered the matter. 'I'm sure it *is* important. But it would be nice if he could have the day off. His boss won't let him, though. He doesn't believe in giving time off for Christmas.'

'He's entitled to a day off,' Charlie said. 'If it were me I'd refuse to work on Christmas day.'

'He'd lose his job if he did that. Mother calls his boss a skinflint.' Timothy returned his attentions to the tree. 'What are those parcels for?'

There was a small pile of packages under the tree, each wrapped in brown paper and tied with string. Charlie noticed them for the first time. 'Presents!' He leapt forward and sifted through them, checking the label on each one. He lifted one up, a large box-shaped parcel, and rattled it. 'Mine!' he shouted.

'Careful,' said his mother. 'It might be breakable.'

'I'm sure it's that toy I saw in Mayfield's shop window,' Charlie said.

Mother was giving nothing away. 'You'll have to wait and see.'

'What are *you* having for Christmas?' Charlie asked his friend.

Timothy shrugged. 'We don't have…actual…presents,' he said. 'Last year I had a bag of peppermint drops. And an orange,' he added.

Charlie and his mother exchanged a look.

Suddenly the front door burst open and Charlie's father entered the house. He took off his hat and removed his cloak with a flourish. 'Aha, the Christmas tree. The latest symbol of high society.' He walked over to his wife and kissed her on the cheek. He stood for a moment, admiring the tree. 'A very fine job you've made of it, my dear, a very fine job indeed.'

She looked pleased. 'We shall be the envy of everyone.'

Her husband nodded in agreement. 'Our social standing this Christmas will go right to the very top. We shall be the talk of street. I shall get in two bottles of vintage port to refresh the expected influx of visitors.'

Charlie coughed politely. 'Have you had a good day, father?'

'Hello, Charlie. Yes I've had an extraordinarily good day. And what's this I see? You've brought home a companion. So tell me, who is this young gentleman?'

'It's Timothy,' Charlie said. 'He lives at the other end of Bayham Street. His father holds an important post and has to work on Christmas Day.'

'Does he indeed? Now that's what I call important.' He took the boy's hand and shook it enthusiastically. 'You must be very proud of your father, young Timothy.'

The boy looked bemused. 'Yes, sir, that I am, sir. Do you ever have to work on Christmas Day, sir?'

'Not that I can recall at the moment. Naturally my post in the Pay Office of His Majesty's Navy is a responsible position, but so far

I have contrived to avoid working on Christmas Day.'

His wife collapsed in a fit of laughter. 'I can't remember the last time you turned in for work at all during the whole week surrounding Christmas Day!'

'It is hardly my fault that my body seems to succumb to illness each year.' He sat down. 'Such talk makes me feel faint. Bring me a glass to revive me.'

'A glass, dear? Pray, what would you be wanting with a glass?'

'You know very well what I mean. Bring me a glass of ale this instant or I shall not be responsible for my actions.'

His wife laughed. 'Is that a promise?'

He leapt to his feet and chased her into the kitchen, him laughing and her cackling.

Timothy gave Charlie a bewildered look.

Charlie shook his head. 'Why do adults have to behave so childishly? Come on, let's go back outside.'

Half an hour later they were staring into the window of Mayfield and Sons, the toyshop in Hampstead Road. Several oil lamps had been placed at strategic positions inside the window to illuminate the toys on sale.

Charlie pointed to a puppet theatre at the centre of the display. 'I wish I'd seen that before. I'd have asked for it for Christmas.'

'I bet it costs a fortune,' Timothy said. 'Would you really be allowed a present like that?'

'Probably not, but there's no harm in asking.' He turned to his friend. 'Your parents *will* buy you a present, won't they?'

Timothy shook his head. 'We'll still have a good time, all the family together.'

'But your father will be at work.'

'He'll be home in the evening. It'll be special.'

Charlie didn't say anything, but he was appalled. Timothy's Christmas Day sounded worse than any *normal* day to him. There was nothing at all special about it.

Around ten o'clock on Christmas morning, Charlie was lighting the candles that adorned their tree.

'Well done, Charlie,' his mother said. 'Your father has insisted that our home is the most festive in the whole street. The vicar and his wife will be calling any moment. If you behave yourself, you can open your present after they leave.' There was a sharp rap at the door. She patted both sides of her hair, just above her ears. 'Here they are now, I'll let them in.'

It wasn't the vicar and his wife. It was young Timothy.

Charlie's mother smiled. 'Happy Christmas, Timothy. You've called for your sugar cane, no doubt.'

Timothy grinned. 'I'm so excited, I just had to show you. I've had a present.'

'That's wonderful.'

'I've got it here.' He held out a large box. 'It was on the table when I came downstairs this morning. It had a label on with my name. Mother said it's a mystery where it came from.'

Charlie walked over. 'Go on then, what is it?'

Timothy opened the lid. 'Look.'

There was a wooden boat, painted bright red. Alongside were twenty or more pairs of small wooden animals.

'A Noah's Ark!' Charlie said.

His mother looked a touch puzzled. 'But that's…'

'It's the first Christmas present I've ever had,' Timothy said. 'I shall treasure it for the rest of my life. Have you opened your present yet, Charlie?'

'We're expecting the vicar to call. Mother says I'm allowed to open my present after he's gone.'

'I'd better be going, too. I just wanted to show you my Noah's Ark.'

Charlie's mother removed a sugar cane from the Christmas tree and handed it to him. 'Happy Christmas, Timothy.'

As soon as the young lad had gone, she turned to her son. 'Charlie, that was *your* Noah's Ark, wasn't it? You gave him *your* present.'

'His family are so poor, Mum. I felt sorry for him.'

She put her arm around him. 'You're a good boy Charlie. That's the real spirit of Christmas. And Timothy is such a weak-looking child. He's so tiny.'

'Tiny. That's right. I shall call him Tiny Tim. One day everyone will know his name.'

'And I suppose everyone will know your name, too.'

'Of course.'

She rubbed his head affectionately. 'You are a dreamer, Charlie Dickens.'

LUSCIOUS

Laura tried to concentrate as she listened to him explaining her duties. She was to be in the office each morning by eight-thirty; open the post, sort it, distribute it. 'It's not a large practice,' he was saying. 'Three solicitors and a couple of conveyancing clerks.' He went on to outline the computer system. It was a lot for Laura to take in. 'Think you can cope with that?' he asked gently.

'I think so, Jon...er...Mr...'

'Please, call me Jonathan. We shall be seeing a lot of each other.'

Laura smiled, trying not to stare at him. Late-twenties, a couple of years older than her. Tall and slim; dark, wavy, luscious hair. And his eyes...

'Right,' he was saying, 'if there's nothing more, I'll show you into the main office and you can make a start. I'll put you with Samantha.'

'Thank you, Jonathan.'

'Yes, you'll like Samantha.' He opened the door and ushered her through. 'She's my fiancée.'

The words hit Laura like a slap round the face. She was certain she wasn't going to like Samantha at all.

She spent the next two hours sorting a large box of filing, while Samantha parked her shapely bottom on an executive swivel-chair and chatted endlessly on the phone. She was the typical vivacious redhead, confident and bossy. Laura found her nasal whine irritating.

'If you've finished the filing there are some contracts to type,' she droned. 'It's lovely having someone to do all my menial tasks.'

The morning passed quickly. Laura glanced up at the clock on the office wall. 'What do you do for lunch?' she asked.

Samantha looked smug. 'I'm popping into town with Jon. I expect he'll treat me to lunch.' She polished the solitaire diamond on her finger. 'I'm looking for an outfit for the office Christmas do.'

'Christmas do?'

'A week on Friday. You can bring your boyfriend.'

'I don't have a boyfriend.'

Samantha smiled. 'Well, well, what a surprise,' she said.

The jibe had touched a sensitive nerve. Laura had never had a boyfriend. It wasn't that she was bad-looking, in fact she'd often been told she was pretty. No, it was simply that for the past ten years all her spare time had been taken nursing her alcoholic mother. It had been hell.

Growing up without the benefit of a father had been hard enough, but watching her mother drink herself into an early grave was something else. Well, she could put it behind her now. Her mother had battled with drink, and the drink had won. It was time for Laura to get a life.

Laura's second day at work was much the same as the first. The morning flew by, and Samantha was every bit as unpleasant. At lunchtime, Laura walked into the town centre and looked in the Christmas shop windows. She had no presents to buy, but it was a good exercise for uplifting the spirits. She resolved to buy a Christmas tree at the weekend, then headed into the *Crusty Loaf* for coffee and a sandwich.

'Come over here and sit with me,' said a friendly voice. It was Jonathan.

Laura nearly dropped her tray. 'Thank you. Samantha's not with you?' she asked hopefully.

'I left her in a shoe shop. She'll be ages yet. Hope she's not too long though, I have to meet the auditors at two-thirty. So, how are you settling in?'

She unloaded her tray and sat opposite him. 'Quite well, I think.'

'Good. Has Samantha mentioned the Christmas do? You can bring your boyfriend.'

Laura purposefully avoided the bright blue eyes across the table. 'I don't have a boyfriend,' she said.

'I'm sorry, I just assumed…'

I've never had a boyfriend, she wanted to say. *Twenty-five and never been kissed.* 'I don't mind going on my own,' she said. 'How long have you and Samantha been together?'

'Almost a year. We've been engaged for three months.'

'That's really nice.' The words sounded hollow. Probably because they were.

Jonathan leaned forward. 'I feel comfortable talking to you. Can I tell you something in confidence?'

Laura's heartbeat moved up a gear. 'Of course you can.'

He glanced over his shoulder before speaking. 'Between you and me, getting engaged to Samantha is the best thing I've ever done.'

She put her sandwich back on the plate. How could she answer that? Luckily, she didn't have to. A nasal voice cut through the silence. 'You two look cosy. Mind if I intrude?'

'Of course not, darling,' Jonathan said. 'Come and join us. We were talking about the Christmas do.'

Samantha sat down and spoke to him as though they were on their own. 'Poor Laura has nobody to go with. She hasn't got a boyfriend.'

'Yes, she told me.'

'You'd think she could find somebody to take her. I mean, she's not *that* bad-looking.'

Laura snapped. 'Excuse me, I do have friends you know. I could easily find a partner for the Christmas night out.'

Samantha turned round, smiling triumphantly. 'Oh, that's wonderful,' she said. 'I'd hate to think you had to come all on your own. We'll really look forward to meeting him, won't we, Jon?'

'We certainly will.'

Laura stared down at her half-eaten sandwich. Damn, she thought. Me and my big mouth.

The smartly-dressed woman at the *Mate-For-Life* dating agency tapped away at her keyboard for a moment, then looked up and smiled.

'Right, Laura, we've fed in all *your* details. Now we need some information about the qualities you're looking for in a *partner.*'

'Late-twenties, tall and slim,' Laura replied with indecent haste. 'Bright blue eyes, and dark, wavy, luscious hair.'

'Right. Very specific, I must say, so far as appearance goes. Let's work through my checklist. How do you feel about men with moustaches?'

'I'm allergic to them.'

'Smoker or non-smoker?'

Laura shook her head. 'No, he doesn't smoke.'

'You're being very definite. You seem to have somebody particular in mind.'

'I have a fair idea of the man I'd like.'

'That's always a help. Good. Let's process your application and see how near we get to your ideal man. We've had great success in the past. Many of the couples we've introduced are now happily married.'

'Brilliant.'

The printer burst into action, spewing out a few lines on a sheet of A4. The smartly-dressed woman read it through. 'Ah yes. Wayne. I remember this young man. Very promising. We may have struck gold.' She handed the sheet of paper to Laura. 'Give him a call and arrange a date. We recommend somewhere busy, like a pub, for your first meeting.'

Laura wondered why she hadn't tried this before. 'That's all there is to it?'

'Easy, isn't it? Let's hope Wayne fulfils your expectations.'

Laura entered the bar of the *Rose and Crown* at exactly eight o'clock. This was the first time she'd ever been in a pub on her own.

There was no sign of Wayne at the tables to her left. She looked across at the bar and suddenly, as if by magic, there he was! Sitting at the bar with his back to her, but even so she was absolutely certain he was her date. His hair was unmistakably dark, wavy and luscious. The dating agency had worked a miracle. She approached, trying to look casual, while her heart was beating like a drum. She could tell he was slim, just like...well, just like she'd hoped. Samantha could keep Jonathan, Laura had found her own hunk! Just as she reached him, he swivelled round.

'Laura, how lovely to see you.'

So that was why he looked like Jonathan. He was Jonathan! She wanted to speak but her voice wouldn't work.

'Can I buy you a drink?' he asked. 'You look as if you need one.'

'I think I do,' she croaked. 'Are you here to meet someone?'

'Of course I am.'

'You're not wearing a buttonhole.'

'Are you all right, Laura? You haven't been drinking?'

'I wish I had. Are you meeting Samantha?'

'Of course. Here she is now.'

Laura wanted to disappear but there was no way of avoiding Samantha. She came bouncing up to Jonathan, kissed him on the cheek and handed over a small parcel. 'A little present for you, as promised.' She turned to Laura. The smile on her face was clearly forced. 'Well, well, look who it is,' she whined. 'Surely you're not on your own? Not when you have all those friends you told us about.'

At that precise moment, Laura noticed a short, chubby young man heading towards her. He had a rose pinned to the top corner of his sweater. As he approached she could see he had brown eyes. His hair was fair, straight, and most definitely *not* luscious.

He looked at the rose pinned to her shirt. 'Hello, Laura. Sorry I'm late.'

She looked at his moustache. 'Wayne?'

'The very same. Now then, let me buy you a drink.'

Jonathan interrupted. 'Come on, Laura, introduce us to your friend.'

'Oh yes, I'm sorry. This is my boyfriend, Wayne.'

Wayne looked pleased to be addressed as her boyfriend. Up to this meeting, he and Laura had only shared a two minute phone conversation.

'Pleased to meet you, Wayne,' said Jonathan. 'Let's make up a foursome. You don't mind, Samantha?'

She yawned. 'If that's what you want.'

They bought drinks and moved to a table. Jonathan sat next to Samantha, and Wayne sat on a bench alongside Laura. He took a large swig of lager and placed his hand firmly on Laura's knee.

'Do you mind?' she said, lifting his hand away.

'I thought I was your boyfriend?'

Samantha laughed. 'What's it like going out with an ice maiden?'

'I think I'll stick some music on the jukebox,' Wayne said.

Samantha stood up. 'I'll join you.' The pair of them headed over to the other side of the bar.

Jonathan looked across at Laura. 'You and Wayne? Is it serious?'

She decided that honesty was the best policy. 'I met him for the first time five minutes ago, when he walked in here.'

'I don't understand.'

'We made contact through a dating agency. This is our first date, and somehow, I don't think it's going to be a great success. Good thing I won't be needing a partner for the office Christmas do.'

'What do you mean by that?'

'You won't like this, but it's Samantha. I can't stand her. I'm leaving the job.'

'There's no need for that.'

'Sorry, Jonathan, I've made up my mind.'

'You don't understand. Samantha no longer works for us.'

Laura couldn't believe her ears. 'That's marvellous. How come?'

'I can't go into details. Confidentiality and all that. If I just say *auditors' report* and *misappropriation of funds...*'

'What, Samantha? I don't believe it.'

'Obviously she had to go.'

'But that's absolutely wonderful. Oh, sorry, I'm forgetting you're engaged.'

'When I first met Samantha, I thought she was terrific. Nothing was too much trouble. After our engagement, she changed. She stopped making any effort. I saw the real person she was.

And that was before I knew she was capable of embezzlement.'

'But you told me getting engaged to her was the best thing you'd ever done.'

'Precisely. I was about to explain to you the other lunchtime, before she interrupted us. Getting engaged made me realise what a mistake it all was.'

'Mistake?'

'Me and Samantha are finished. We agreed to meet here tonight to return our engagement rings.' He glanced towards the jukebox. 'She doesn't seem too heartbroken.'

'And what about you, Jonathan? Are you heartbroken?'

'I will be if you don't agree to be my partner at the Christmas do.'

Laura smiled. 'Nothing would make me happier.'

He leaned forward and kissed her lightly on the lips. She closed her eyes, pulled him even closer, and ran her fingers through his dark, wavy, luscious hair.

THREE VIEWS OF CHRISTMAS

FIRST VIEW

'I'll finish up these roast potatoes,' Gran said as she emptied out the serving dish onto her plate.

Rory stared open-mouthed. 'But I haven't had...' he started, but Mum's interruption cut him short.

'It's good to see you enjoying your Christmas dinner, Gran,' she said.

'Greedy cow,' Rory muttered under his breath. Then he cast his mother a jubilant grin as he said loudly, 'You must come to stay more often, Gran. Not just at Christmas.'

43

Dad choked, struggling to contain the forkful of turkey he had just placed in his mouth. Mum looked furious. 'Go and fetch your father a glass of water,' she snapped.

Rory went out to the kitchen. He couldn't understand why they didn't tell Gran not to be so selfish. The fact that she was old and useless was no reason to toady to her the way they did. It would serve them right if she *did* visit more frequently. He took a drinking glass from the wall cupboard. On second thoughts, he wouldn't suggest that again. He couldn't stand Gran either.

Thank God he was going away tomorrow. A broad grin spread over his face. A dirty grin. *Kirsty.* He held the glass under the cold tap. This was going to be his best Christmas ever. A week in Newquay with Kirsty. That should end the year with a bang.

He jumped as a stream of cold water ran down his shirt sleeve.

'Would you like a *Quality Street*, Gran?' Rory asked, handing over the half-empty tin.

'Thought you'd never ask,' she grumbled. 'Huh. Not much of a selection left. All the hazelnut toffees have gone.' She pulled out three sweets with her chubby fingers.

'I see you managed to find one you like,' Rory said.

Gran was too busy munching to answer. *Pig*, he thought. *Funny she doesn't share HER chocolates*. He knew she'd been given at least two boxes as Christmas presents. Her selfishness really wound him up. He almost wished he'd stayed in the kitchen and helped Mum and Dad wash up.

He looked sideways at her. God, she was huge. The only time she exerted any energy was when she was eating. Rory had often heard his parents talking about her, complaining that she'd always been lazy. Apparently, Gramps used to do everything for her. That's why he'd only lasted into his sixties. Gran was well into her eighties and as strong as an ox. These days she had a home help, meals brought in, neighbours to do the shopping. Rory sighed. And every Christmas with us.

'Enjoying your Christmas, Gran?' he said loudly.

'Wouldn't say *no* to a drop of sherry,' she said.

He found himself chuckling as he poured her a generous glassful. You had to admire her cheek. 'I'm going away tomorrow,' he said. 'Taking my girlfriend to Newquay for a few days.' He handed Gran the glass, adding with a wink, 'She's promised to give me a Christmas treat while we're away.'

Gran took a large gulp. 'Make sure you behave yourself. There's no telling what you youngsters get up to these days.'

'Get on. I bet you used to be a devil when you were younger.'

Gran gave a wistful smile. 'We had our moments. Not the way you lot carry on of course.' She took another drink. 'Is the Queen on yet?'

'Sorry, Gran, you've missed her. We've been watching Channel 4.'

'Huh. I wondered what this rubbish was.'

She sat there for the next half-hour. Rory assumed she was sulking. At various times she belched, snored and farted. He decided it was time to sneak away.

She sat up before he reached the door. 'Off out, are you?'

'Thought I'd see if I could be any help in the kitchen,' he lied.

Gran pulled something from her handbag. 'Here, I'd like you to have this,' she said.

SECOND VIEW

Bit stingy for a Christmas dinner, Gran thought. *If you can't have a good blowout at Christmas, when can you?* She glared over at Rory's plate. They'd definitely given him more turkey than they'd given her.

Gran surveyed the table. The sprouts had all gone. The gravy boat was empty. She craned her head and peered into the vegetable dish. There were two roast potatoes left.

47

'I'll clear up these,' she said, scraping the contents onto her plate. She'd have to be careful. Too many vegetables always gave her terrible wind.

Christine was saying something to her but she couldn't hear properly. It was difficult to hear when you were eating. Gran didn't care. It was bound to be something patronising, coming from Christine. Gran had never taken to her. She always looked so mean and pinched. Mike could have done so much better for himself.

She popped the last roaster into her mouth. Rory was saying something about having Gran over to visit more often, not just at Christmas. Well, there's a surprise.

Mike suddenly choked on his turkey. Gran thought he looked ill. But then he was so thin. Almost emaciated. Christine didn't look after him properly.

What was Rory bringing him now? A glass of water. Typical. He wasn't going to get very fat on that.

Gran sat on the settee, thinking. There was nothing wrong with her mind. She *didn't* imagine things.

Things *had* gone missing. Gradually, one at a time. It had started with the contents of her jewel box. Then it was the Staffordshire figurines. Napoleon had been the first to go. Then Shakespeare. There was nothing left now, apart from Nelson. He was by far the most valuable piece. Gran knew he would have gone as well if she hadn't hidden him in the oven.

She'd sacked the home help of course. The social worker hadn't liked that. That's why they were putting her in a home. *Sunnybanks*, they called it. *Huh*. She didn't want to go. She liked her little cottage. But she didn't have any say in the matter. Her mind was unstable, that's what they'd said.

She'd decided to give Nelson to Mike and Christine as a thank-you for looking after her over Christmas. It would be a surprise for them at the end of her stay. She'd brought him with her in her suitcase, wrapped in newspaper. She didn't want to leave him in her case all over Christmas, so she needed to hide him somewhere. They'd put her in the spare room, which had a lovely old-fashioned wardrobe in the corner. That was just the job. She'd hide Nelson on the top.

That's how she'd discovered them. All her other Staffordshire figures, hidden on top of the wardrobe.

Rory wasn't a bad lad when you got to know him. He'd sat with her on the settee, given her chocolates and a glass of sherry. He'd chatted with her, told her he was going to Newquay with his girlfriend. Gran came to a decision. She took Nelson from her handbag.

'Here,' she said to Rory. 'I'd like you to have this.'

Rory looked shell-shocked. He took the small figurine in his hands and examined it. 'Thanks, Gran,' he said. 'It's nice.'

'I know it's not your kind of thing. But it's worth a few bob. Sell it. Then I want you to promise me something.'

'Anything you like, Gran.'

'Firstly, don't give any of the money to your mother or father.'

Rory smiled. 'You didn't need ask me that, Gran. But anyway, I promise.'

'And secondly, while you're in Newquay, take that girl of yours to the Atlantic Hotel. Buy her a cream tea.'

'Been there yourself, have you, Gran?'

She nodded and blinked away a tear. 'A long time ago. We had the honeymoon suite.' She squeezed Rory's hand. 'Will you do that for me?'

'Course I will. Anything else?'

'Pour us another glass of sherry,' she said.

THIRD VIEW

Mike picked up the saucepan from the draining-board and began wiping it. 'Nice having Mum to stay at Christmas, isn't it?'

Christine glared at him. 'I'm glad you think so. Personally, I'm delighted this is the last time we'll be having her.'

Mike looked puzzled. 'What d'you mean, the last time?'

'Obvious, isn't it? Once she moves into the home, she won't need to come here. *Sunnybanks* can have the pleasure of her.'

'You can't mean that.'

'Oh can't I? She's impossible. Greedy, selfish. And now her memory's gone.'

'She's my mother,' Mike said. 'And she's not that bad. Just because she forgot she'd given you those Staffordshire figures.'

'Yes, and accused everybody else of stealing them from her. The woman's a menace.'

Mike shook his head. 'We'll all be old sometime. It can't be very pleasant for her, having to move out of the house she's known all her life. The council will probably force her to sell her cottage to pay the fees of *Sunnybanks*.'

Christine looked concerned. 'Can they do that?'

'Oh yes. She's only allowed to hang on to a certain amount of capital. Her cottage is worth far more than that. It's very sad.' Mike hung up the wiping-up cloth on its hook. 'I'll go and check she's all right. She's in the lounge with Rory.'

Christine slumped down at the kitchen table. *He thinks it's sad they'll sell her cottage. Sad? It's a bloody tragedy. Our inheritance, gone. The inheritance is the only reason I've stuck with him all these years.*

She laughed unfeelingly. *Mike is such a prat. He actually believed his stupid mother gave me those Staffordshire figures. Good job I did take them. It doesn't look as if the old bag will be leaving us anything else.*

THE HOLLY COTTAGE MYSTERY

'It's definitely the same cottage,' Craig said, opening out the brochure on the table and pressing it flat to display the photo. 'You'd have to be stupid not to see that.'

Karen narrowed her eyes at him. 'Thank you very much,' she said, trying to sound hurt. She gave a thin smile. 'Don't get me wrong, I can see there are similarities. The stonework looks the same, and the doorway is the same shape. It's a totally different door, though. Come on, Craig, there must be thousands of cottages with this kind of frontage.'

Craig picked up a battered six-by-four black-and-white snapshot from the shelf and placed it on the table next to the illustration in the brochure. His blue eyes were twinkling proudly. 'Compare the two photos. Look carefully. Do you see it now?'

Karen looked hard at the old snapshot, then turned her attention to the picture in the holiday brochure. She shook her head. 'Not really. I fail to see how you can be so certain. It's doubly difficult because your Mum's old photo is black-and-white, and the modern brochure is in colour. And it doesn't help that, in the old photo, your Mum is standing in front of the door holding you in her arms. I'm sorry, hun, but if I'm honest, I think you're imagining things.'

'Concentrate your attention on the stone lintel above the doorway,' Craig said. 'Then tell me I'm making it up.'

She reluctantly cast her eyes once more over the photos. And suddenly stopped in her tracks. 'Oh yes. I think I can see what you're getting at. It's a pity the pictures aren't bigger.'

Craig handed her the large magnifying glass he'd been using earlier. 'Once you look at it through this, you'll see it's beyond doubt.'

Karen focussed her eyes through the magnifying glass, first on the old photo, then on the new.

'Have I ever told you how attractive you look when you're concentrating?' Craig asked.

'Yeah, right.'

He kissed her cheek. 'No, really, I mean it. Now, what can you see?'

She looked up. 'That's amazing. Incredible. The date carved on the stone lintel. 1836. And unquestionably the same carving. The top circle of the eight is lop-sided, and the loop of the six is bent and projects high above the other numbers.'

'Exactly.' Craig was grinning now, and there was a note of triumph in his voice. 'Once you see it, there's no doubt.'

'It's the same lintel in both photos, too,' Karen said. 'It's wider on the right-hand side. This is absolutely fantastic. How on earth did you spot it, though? How did you realise that the two photos were of the same cottage?'

He picked up the old snapshot. 'This is the only link I have with my Mum. The only thing that's survived. All I know about her is that she died when I was three years old, and I was put up for adoption. I know every square millimetre of this photo, by heart. The front of that old cottage is as real to me as if I'd lived there my whole life. The way that date is inscribed on that lintel is kind of burnt into my brain. I'd know it anywhere. So when I saw the photo in the holiday brochure, it leapt straight out at me. Shouted at me. *Mum's cottage.'*

'And where *is* this cottage?'

'It says in the brochure it's in Wiltshire. A village called Great Somerford.'

'Sounds lovely. The sort of place where you might meet Miss Marple. So what happens next?'

Craig turned over the old snapshot and read out the faded inscription that his mother had written on the back. '*Me with Craig. Holly Cottage. Xmas 1978.'*

'Yes, you would have just turned three.' Karen took the photo and turned it back over. 'You actually looked cute at that age.'

'You cheeky little…'

She kissed him on the nose, then took another look at the photo. 'Your Mum was a bit of a looker, wasn't she? I suppose she'd have been in her early twenties when this was taken.'

Craig nodded. 'Something like that. I obviously inherited my good looks from her, don't you think?'

'If you say so.' Karen smiled and put the photo back on the table. 'Am I to assume you've checked how far it is to Great Somerford?'

'We could be there in an hour and a half. I've been thinking...'

'Now there's a surprise.'

'The thing is, the reason I picked up this holiday brochure in the first place was to find a cottage we could rent over Christmas. Just the two of us. It would be great to get away from it all and relax for a couple of weeks.'

'I think I can see where this is going.'

'Holly Cottage looks ideal. It's been modernised, and there's a wood-burner too. And Great Somerford looks a quaint little village.'

'And we could ask around the locals to see if anybody remembers your Mum?'

'It's forty years since she lived there, but somebody might. You don't mind, do you? I'd dearly like to discover a bit more about her.'

Karen put her hand gently on his shoulder. 'Of course I don't mind. It might be a lot of fun. Just don't get your hopes up too much though. The chances of finding somebody who actually remembers your Mum are pretty slim. And besides, Christmas is only a month away and most likely the cottage is already booked up.'

'It *is* booked up over Christmas,' Craig said, then added brightly. 'I reserved it earlier this afternoon.'

It was just after four o'clock on the twentieth of December when Craig steered their trusty Volkswagen Golf off the M4 at the Chippenham roundabout. Dusk was already setting in, and dark clouds in the sky threatened an imminent snowfall. 'About four miles of country lanes to go and we'll be there,' he said.

'I have a good feeling about this,' Karen said. 'This is going to be a wonderful Christmas. I hope our holiday cottage lives up to expectations.'

Great Somerford was everything they'd wished for, the quintessential English village. The main street was flanked with pretty cottages with gates and neat front gardens. Craig slowed down to a crawl as he passed the village shop and a row of allotments.

'According to the directions, this should be it,' he said, pulling up opposite the Volunteer Inn. 'There it is. Holly Cottage.'

'It looks so sweet,' Karen said.

'Just like in Mum's photo.' Craig pulled onto the drive and was out of the car in a second. He put the key into the front door lock and turned the handle. 'Strange to think I was here thirty-odd years ago.'

Karen followed him out of the car. 'Any memories coming back to you? Any bells ringing?'

'None at all.' Craig opened the door and stepped inside, Karen following close behind.

The front door led straight into the living room, and she stood gazing around the room, taking it all in. It was a good-sized room, tastefully decorated in neutral colours, and well-furnished. A comfortable-looking three-piece-suite, good quality dining table and chairs, and a TV in the corner. Two well-painted country landscapes hung on one of the longer walls. 'What a lovely room,' she said. 'It seems to invite me inside.'

'Brrr,' Craig said.

'Cold?' she asked. 'It feels warm in here to me.' She placed her hand next to the storage heater. 'Yes, the heating's on.'

'It's not so much the temperature. More a feeling. Something's given me the shivers.'

'Let's check out the rest of the cottage, and then have a cuppa. That's what's called for.'

Upstairs were two bedrooms, one spacious, the other cot-sized, and a bathroom with all the necessaries. All clean and fresh. Back downstairs, the kitchen was compact, but well fitted-out. Modern units, a decent cooker and microwave.

Ten minutes later they were sitting on the sofa together with a cup of tea and a packet of chocolate digestives.

'Better now?' Karen asked.

'Much better. Cosy, isn't it?'

'It's a lovely cottage. Has it awoken any memories of when you were here as a three-year-old?'

'None whatsoever. It's as new to me as it is to you.'

She squeezed his hand. 'It's wonderful to get away from everything. We have two whole weeks to ourselves.'

'I'm sorely tempted to switch off my phone. I've told everyone in the office that I'm away, so they won't be expecting me to pick up.'

'Great idea. Do it.'

'I will.' He took his phone from his pocket. 'How about you? Could you bring yourself to disconnect from the rest of civilisation? For a couple of weeks?'

Karen thought for a moment. 'It's funny when you say it like that. Makes it seem a big deal. Hmm. But there's no reason why anybody from the hospital is likely to call me, either.

'You deserve a break. Yours is a high-pressure job.'

'I must admit I'm ready for a break. If anybody wants to see their psychoanalyst over Christmas, I'm afraid this one is unavailable.'

'I'm so pleased to hear you say that.'

'Anyway, I could always check my phone once a day, just in case I'd missed an important message.' She fished her phone from her bag. 'Yes, I'm switching mine off, too.' She raised the palm of her hand towards his, and they high-fived.

'Here's to a proper relaxing break,' Craig said. 'And perhaps…?'

Karen smiled. 'Perhaps. We'll see.'

They finished drinking their tea and then unpacked their cases. Craig set about lighting the wood-burning stove.

'You still feeling cold?' Karen asked.

'I can't understand it. I was fine while I was upstairs unpacking my clothes, but as soon as I came down here, I'm shivering like I'm suffering from the DT's.'

'But it's warmer down here than it is upstairs.'

'I know. I don't think it has anything to do with the temperature.'

'But it happened as you came downstairs?'

Craig thought for a second. 'That's right.' He walked over to the bottom of the staircase.

'Something…yes, it's here. Something…I can't explain it. I simply feel very uncomfortable standing here.'

'There has to be a logical explanation.' She joined him at the foot of the stairs. 'I think I've got it. There's a cupboard here, under the stairs. The door to it is closed, but what's the betting the cupboard has some kind of a vent that leads to outside? That's why it's making you feel cold.' She reached for the door handle.

'Don't open it!' Craig shouted desperately.

'It's just a cupboard. It can't hurt you. What are you afraid of?'

'I have no idea. This is weird. It's that cupboard, though. That's what's upsetting me. It's giving me a bad feeling. I don't want you to open the door to it.'

'That *is* weird. We need to get to the bottom of this, to prove to you there is nothing here for you to fear. Go back upstairs out of the way, and I'll take a look inside the cupboard.'

'No. Just leave it.'

'Craig, we can't ignore this. There is no way we can spend the next two weeks here, wondering why this cupboard is giving you the spooks. Now, take a good deep breath and try to keep calm.'

He did as she said, slowing his breathing right down. 'You're absolutely right,' he said. 'Go on, open that door. I'll be all right.'

Karen didn't wait to give him time to change his mind. She turned the handle and opened the door. She'd been expecting a blast of cold air to hit her, but there was no hint of any change in temperature. Inside the cupboard were a broom, a mop and bucket, and a vacuum cleaner. Nothing too threatening, unless you were allergic to housework. 'There, just a normal cupboard under the stairs,' she said, turning to face him.

His face was noticeably pale. 'I don't know what's got into me. Let me see in there.'

Karen stood aside. 'Well done, that's the best way of dealing the problem. Confront it.'

Craig stood at the entrance. 'It's really strange. I felt I wanted to climb up a step into the cupboard, but there isn't one. The floor level in the cupboard is the same as in the hallway.'

'This is starting to make some kind of sense. Coming here today has awakened your memory of when you were here before as a toddler. I think your brain can remember climbing up a step into that cupboard all those years ago. And since you're feeling so uncomfortable about looking in the cupboard, it's my guess that your memories are unpleasant ones.'

'I take it you're speaking to me now in your capacity as a psychoanalyst?'

'You don't mind, do you?'

'Of course not. It's just that I have no recollection of ever being here before.'

'No conscious recollections. But your brain knows, and it's trying to tell you.'

'You really think so?'

'I do. I don't want to upset you, Craig, but I think you were shut in that cupboard when you were a kid, probably as a punishment for some reason or other. And that's why you now feel so distressed when you're in this area of the cottage.'

'It's possible I suppose. Funnily enough, now you've explained it I don't feel so upset.'

'Excellent. I'm taking that as a result.'

'I wonder why I was shut in the cupboard, though?'

Karen grinned. 'You were obviously a naughty little boy. Some things don't change. Now, shouldn't we be thinking about supper?'

Craig peered out of the window. 'The lights have come on at the Volunteer Inn. They're bound to do food of some description. And, hey, it's starting to snow.'

'How lovely.' She kissed his cheek. 'The Christmas holiday starts here.'

The Volunteer was exactly the kind of pub you'd hope to find in an English village. Timber panelling, oak beams, and a roaring log fire. The large, central bar looked well-stocked with bottles, optics and glasses, and was run by Old Jim, a weather-beaten man of indeterminate age. His tousled hair probably hadn't seen a comb or a pair of scissors for months, and his bushy sideburns grew freely down the sides of his face like a rampant creeper on the outside of a house. He had a ruddy complexion, most especially on his cheeks and his nose.

'Aha,' he said, greeting Craig and Karen with a smile as they entered the pub, 'newcomers to the village. Are you staying hereabouts, or have you come in here simply to shelter from the snow?'

'We're staying just across the road. Holly Cottage,' Craig said. 'We're here for the next two weeks.'

'Cosy little house,' said Old Jim. 'What can I get you to drink?'

Craig had a pint of Arkell's 3B, and Karen a large gin and tonic. They carried their drinks over to the table nearest to the open fire, and sat down to study the menu. It was quiet for a Saturday night with only a couple of other drinkers in the bar, but it was early yet.

'The Landlord looks like he's been running this place for centuries,' Craig said. 'I'm going to ask him if he remembers my Mum.'

Karen nudged him. 'Don't rush it. Take your time and keep your ears open. More locals are bound to come in soon and we might get an opportunity to chat to them. I'm a great believer in fate, and if we allow the opportunity to arise, I believe it will.'

A pretty teenaged waitress came over and took their order for food. Craig went for rib-eye steak with hand-cut chips, and Karen the fish pie with seasonal vegetables. While they were waiting for their food to arrive a man of around sixty wandered over and stood next to the fire, warming his hands. He was dressed in jeans and a sweater, a stocky chap but not overweight. He was carrying a pint of bitter and took a swig before he turned and spoke to them.

'Chilly tonight,' he said. 'The sky looks full of snow. I'm supposed to be working on Monday but I have a feeling my Christmas break has already started.'

'It sounds as though you work outside,' Karen said. 'Let me guess. A builder?'

'Clever girl, got it in one,' he said with a smile. 'Old Jim tells me you're staying at Holly Cottage over Christmas.'

'I can see word travels quickly around here,' Craig said.

'Jungle drums. You know, the old grapevine. Everybody knows everybody else's business. That's village life for you.' He took a step

70

closer to them and offered out his hand. 'I'm Doug, by the way. I do a fair bit of the building work around the village.'

They shook his hand in turn. 'I suppose there are plenty of odd jobs to be done,' Karen said. 'I mean, there are dozens of very old cottages and they must take a lot of maintaining.'

Doug took another drink of his beer. 'There's always something needs fixing. I do bigger jobs too, sometimes. Matter of fact, I carried out the renovations at Holly Cottage. Be about three years ago. Oh yes, quite a big job that was.'

Craig looked up to speak, but Karen gave him another gentle nudge that said 'leave the talking to me, dear'.

'It looks lovely now,' she said. 'I suppose it was in a bit of a state before you set to work on it?'

'You can say that again. It had been sorely neglected. New bathroom, new kitchen, and redecoration from top to bottom. Even had to replace some of the floors. Took me a fair time, I can tell you. A few months' work all told.'

'I'm sure it was. Tell me, Doug, did you have to replace the floor in the cupboard under the stairs?'

Doug thought about it while he drained the remaining beer from his glass. 'No, as I remember, the floor in that cupboard was okay.'

'So you don't think there was ever a step up into the cupboard?'

If Doug thought it was an odd question he didn't show it. 'Wouldn't have thought so,' he said. 'It wouldn't make sense to have a step into the cupboard. There's little enough headroom as it is.'

Craig couldn't stay out of the conversation any longer. 'Have you lived around these parts long?' he asked.

'Born and bred in the village. There's not much goes on around here that I don't know about.'

'You might be able to help us,' Karen said. 'The reason we chose Holly Cottage for our break is that Craig's mum lived in it for a while. A long time ago now.'

'Did she indeed? What was her name?'

'This is going to sound funny, but we don't know. She died when Craig was very young, and he was adopted. All we know for certain is that she stayed in Holly Cottage in 1978.'

'1978? That is a long time ago. But surely…?'

'She was there at Christmas time that year,' Craig said. 'I was only three years old at the time, and I was there too.'

Doug's hitherto smiling face had transformed into a concerned frown. He was about to speak when the waitress arrived with the food. 'Tell you what,' he said, 'you two eat your food and I'll have a word with a couple of people in the bar, see if I can find out anything for you. I'll speak to you later.'

'Thank you, Doug.' Karen asked the waitress to get another pint for Doug and charge it to their tab. Then they turned their attention to the food, and Doug made his way over to the drinkers in the bar.

He suddenly seemed less relaxed than he had before.

An hour later, with a decent meal inside them, Craig and Karen settled back in their seats to continue their chat with Doug. Craig wasn't a big beer-drinker but the Arkell's was going down well. 'So, have you managed to find anyone who remembers my Mum?' he asked.

Doug seemed uncomfortable. 'You mentioned that your Mum died when you were young. Do you happen to know what she died of?'

Craig shook his head. 'When I was very young my adoptive parents told me my Mum had died, but they had no other details. All they had was an old black-and-white snapshot of my Mum holding me in her arms outside Holly Cottage. So when I was eighteen I applied to Social Services for information.'

'And what did they tell you?'

'Nothing of any consequence. I hit a brick wall. They had no record of me, or my parents. It seems that my file has vanished into thin air.'

'Typical inefficient bureaucracy. So you came to Great Somerford in the hope of discovering something about your parents?'

'Exactly that. We know my Mum was here with me at Christmastime in 1978. Not sure if my Dad was here or not. It's getting on for forty years ago, but somebody might remember something.'

Doug took another drink from his glass but said nothing.

'Well?' prompted Craig. 'Do you have any information for me?'

Doug nodded, a sombre expression clouding his face. At last he spoke. 'I've just been discussing this with a couple of people in the bar, people who have lived here for as long as I have. Between us we've pieced together some details of your mother's time here in the late seventies.'

'That's wonderful.'

'In 1978, a guy called Ian Rushton lived in Holly Cottage. He'd have been in his twenties at the time, a bit of a rough diamond but very popular with the ladies. Nobody seems to recall what he did for a living, but he rented the cottage from a local family. It was in a pretty poor state of repair in those days, and the rent was cheap. From what I can gather, it seems that sometime during the summer of 1978, your mum moved in with him, bringing her little toddler with her.' Doug pointed his finger at Craig. 'That was you, of course.'

'Well I'm damned. Does anybody remember my mum's name?'

'Rachael Williams. The consensus seems to be that Ian wasn't your father, and I'm afraid I can't shed any light as to who might be.'

'No matter,' Craig said. 'I can't tell you how brilliant it feels to be learning something about my mum at last.'

'Their relationship seems to have been a bit stormy. I'm sorry to have to tell you this, but your mum seems to have liked a drink or two. This is all just hearsay of course, but there are those that feel she neglected you a bit.'

Karen gave Craig's wrist a comforting squeeze. 'Tell us, Doug,' she said, 'do *you* remember Rachael at all? I reckon you'd have been a young lad in your twenties at that time.'

Doug laughed. 'Oh yes, I remember Rachael all right. Any lad my age couldn't help but notice her. She was an absolute cracker. Not that she ever paid any attention to me.'

'She only had eyes for this Ian, is that it?'

'Not sure I'd go so far as to say that. But you know how people gossip, especially in a village.'

'Is this what you were getting at when you said they had a stormy relationship?'

'That, and the drinking. Sorry, but she didn't have the best of reputations.'

Craig scratched his ear. 'It's not your fault, Doug,' he said. 'I came here to find out something of my mum, and I have to accept the bad with the good. Unfortunately it seems to be more bad than good. Isn't there something positive you can tell me about her?'

'Of course. Let's see. Firstly, as I've already mentioned, she was an exceptionally attractive girl. She dressed well and always looked clean and tidy. She spoke well, too. Not exactly posh, but certainly not common. You could tell she was intelligent, just by talking to her. I seem to remember hearing she'd had a good education and had been training to become a teacher. I'm certain she would have done just that, if...'

'...if she hadn't had an illegitimate child,' Craig said. 'Yes, I expect me coming along cramped her style somewhat.'

Doug took another drink from his glass. 'I have no doubt that, had she lived, Rachael would have bounced back career-wise, once you'd grown up a bit. It was a tragedy that her life was cut short the way it was.'

'So what can you tell me about the way she died?' Craig asked. 'Do you have any details?'

Doug nodded. 'It was big news in the village at the time. Sometime early in 1979, we think it was. She was still living at Holly Cottage with Ian. And you, of course. Just a tragic accident, that's all. She tripped down the stairs and unfortunately landed badly at the foot of the staircase. She was already dead by the time the emergency services arrived at the house. Look here, I'm sorry to have to be the one to break this to you.'

'Not at all,' Craig said, 'I knew it wasn't going to be easy, finding out what had happened to Mum. I think the knowledge will help me in the long run. It's far better to know the truth, than to keep speculating as to what might have happened. Do you happen to know what became of Ian Rushton?'

'I'm sorry to say he died not too long afterwards. Drove his motor-bike into a ditch.'

'My God,' Karen said. 'One disaster after another.'

'If you want any further details, there's a chance Michael Scrivener might be able to help you. He runs the butcher's shop just down the road. There was an inquest held into your mother's death, and we think he may have a copy of the local paper that carried the report.'

'After all this time?'

'Local history is a passion of his. Well, he never got married, so that's where he throws his time and energy.' Doug laughed. 'My missus would never allow me to spend all my spare time researching village gossip. I'll phone him in the morning and ask him if he can help you. I'm sure he'll jump at the chance. Give me your number and I'll keep you posted.'

'Right,' Craig said. 'In that case I'd better switch on my phone again.'

'It's been quite a night,' Karen said as they climbed into bed. 'You're a bit quiet, hun. Not surprising, really. It's been a roller coaster for you, hasn't it?'

'It came as a blow to hear that Mum might have neglected me.'

She ran her hand lightly over his forehead. 'It's bound to hurt. Of course, it's only gossip. Chances are there's no truth in it whatsoever.'

'I know.'

'Do you think you've dug deep enough into your past now? Do you think it might be better to leave it?'

'I don't think I can,' Craig said. 'I'm going to have to see this through to the end.'

She stroked the side of his face. 'That's exactly what I expected you to say.' She kissed him lightly on the lips. 'I would feel just the same if it was me.'

Craig turned over and pulled the duvet tightly around him. 'Thanks, beautiful. Goodnight.'

The view from the front window of Holly Cottage the following morning was like a scene on a

Christmas card; thatched cottages, front gardens with gates, the village pub, a red letter box, all topped with two or three inches of snow.

True to his word, Doug phoned Craig just before eleven o'clock to tell him that Michael Scrivener would be pleased to have a chat with them. So, fifteen minutes later, wrapped up warm in coats and scarves and taking care not to slip on the narrow pavement, they made their way carefully along the High Street to the small butcher's shop. Karen tapped on the side door as instructed and they waited for it to be opened.

'Nervous?' she asked Craig.

'Not at all. I feel more positive about things this morning.'

The door opened, and there stood Michael Scrivener. He looked to be somewhere in his mid-sixties, but it was difficult to judge as he'd lost almost all of his hair, and clearly hadn't shaved this morning. His clear blue eyes twinkled though, and Karen had a feeling he might have been a good-looking lad in his youth. They shook hands and introduced themselves, and he led them upstairs to his living quarters above the shop.

The living room was a good size, but hadn't been decorated for a long time. The ceiling was low, and there were two small windows overlooking the street below. The furniture belonged to another age, somewhere in the middle of the twentieth century. He indicated for them to sit down, and Karen was pleasantly surprised to find the settee was comfortable.

'So you are Rachael Williams' boy?' he said to Craig. 'The last time I saw you, your mum had you in her arms while I weighed her out a pound of bacon. And here you are a grown man. It hardly seems possible.'

'Almost forty years ago,' Craig said.

'Quite so, we're none of us getting any younger,' Scrivener said, running a hand over his bald pate. 'I understand you're trying to find out a bit about your mother. How much do you know?'

'Until last night, I didn't even know her name,' Craig said.

'Anything you can tell us will help,' Karen added.

'I'm not sure I can be much use to you, but I'll do my best. Rachael was a very pretty girl, outgoing, intelligent, with a good sense of humour. During the seventies, while you were a very small boy, she lived with Ian Rushton in Holly Cottage. You have to appreciate that people had different ideas in those days as to what was acceptable behaviour. Your mum was living with a man but not married to him, and she had a child, too. Worse still, it seemed likely that Rushton wasn't the father. Nowadays this kind of thing is commonplace, but back then it was frowned upon. Small villages like Great Somerford are full of people with nothing better to do than gossip, and I'm afraid that's what they did when it came to your mum.'

'It's been hinted that she had a drink problem,' Craig said. 'Was that true?'

Michael Scrivener scratched his ear. 'I've heard it said. I never saw her drunk, but I only used to see your mum when she came into my shop, so I really couldn't say.'

'One more thing,' Craig said, his voice wobbling. 'Do you think my mum neglected me?'

'Not to my knowledge. She always brought you into the shop with her, and she seemed really proud of you.' Scrivener smiled. 'And hey, you've grown up into a fine, healthy young man, so she must have done something right.' He tapped Craig gently on the shoulder. 'As I said, villages like this are full of scandalmongers. It doesn't pay to take too much notice of idle gossip.'

'You're right, of course,' Karen said. 'Thank you for taking the time to talk to us.'

Craig nodded, his eyes full.

Michael Scrivener continued. 'My pleasure. I know it all happened a long time ago but I would like to say how sorry I am that your mum died so tragically. I can see you are finding this hard, but hopefully, in the long run, you'll feel better about things.' He turned and picked up a yellowed newspaper from the sideboard. 'On that note, I've looked out this old copy of the *Gazette and Herald* for you to borrow. It carries a report of the inquest into your mum's death. Take it back with you to Holly Cottage and read it at your leisure. It will tell you everything there is to know about your mother's death.'

The newspaper report was disturbing. Written in the style of the period it detailed the events of the day Rachael Williams died, as presented to the Coroner's Court. Ian Rushton gave evidence that Rachael had been very difficult that afternoon and had stormed out of the cottage, leaving their young toddler with him. She had returned several hours later the worse for drink and had gone upstairs without speaking. Ian Rushton remained downstairs looking after the young child. A short while later he had heard noises on the landing and had rushed out to find her lying motionless at the foot of the stairs. He immediately called the emergency services, but it was too late to save her. The local policeman, Terry Smith, gave evidence that supported Ian Rushton's story. It had not been possible to establish where Rachael had been during the time she was out of the house, or where she had obtained the alcohol, although Ian Rushton stated that it was not unusual for her to carry a bottle of gin in her bag. Her doctor gave the cause of death as a broken neck. Unsurprisingly, the court returned a verdict of Accidental Death.

After Craig and Karen had finished reading the report they agreed that their best course of action would be to walk across the road to the Volunteer Inn.

Doug was seated on a stool at the bar and just finishing his first pint of the day when they entered the pub. They bought themselves a drink, and a fresh one for Doug, and sat at the bar with him. He thanked them for the drink. 'How did you get on with Michael Scrivener?' he asked.

'Very well,' Karen said. 'He wasn't able to give us a great deal of information, but he did let us borrow the local newspaper with the report of the inquest. That was interesting.'

'And a bit unsettling,' Craig added.

Old Jim was hovering behind the bar, and chipped in. 'I daresay Michael was able to fill in a few gaps for you about your mum. I mean, if anybody could help you out, it would be him.'

'He did his best, certainly,' Craig said. 'But he couldn't add a great deal to what Doug had already told us. Not surprising really, as he only ever saw my mum when she came into his shop to buy her meat.'

Old Jim stuck his elbow on the bar and chuckled. 'That's what he said, is it?'

Doug put his glass down. 'Funny how some people can't remember things so well when they get older.'

'Are you saying that Michael Scrivener knew my mother better than he was letting on?' Doug said. 'Hang on a minute. Were they having an affair?'

Old Jim leaned closer and kept his voice down. 'Michael Scrivener was absolutely besotted with your mother and there was gossip flying around the village that she used to visit him sometimes. You know, after he'd closed the shop for the day. Whether they were having a full-blown affair is anybody's guess, but I know for a fact he used to carry a photo of your mum around with him. I often used to see it when he opened his wallet to pay for a round of drinks. He carried it for years and years after she'd died. It might still be in his wallet for all I know.'

Karen took a sip of her gin. 'Strange that he didn't think to mention that photo to us.'

'Or to show it to us,' Craig said. 'I'd love to see it, if he's still got it.'

'There's no way he'd have thrown it away,' Old Jim said. 'But don't you go blurting out to him that I told you about it. He can be a touchy old cuss at times, but I don't want to risk losing one of my regular customers.'

'Don't worry, we'll be discrete,' Karen said. 'Now then, I think it's time we took a gander at your Sunday Lunch menu.'

'It was a mistake to come here, raking up the past,' Craig said. 'All we've discovered is that my Mum was a boozer, and that she neglected me.'

They were back in Holly Cottage, having consumed a delicious roast lunch and several rounds of drinks.

'That's a ridiculously negative way of viewing the situation,' Karen said. 'There's absolutely no evidence to show that you were neglected as a child.'

'I'm being realistic, that's all. If anything, I'm understating how bad it was. You were the one who said I was probably locked in that cupboard under the stairs as some kind of a punishment. I was three years old, for crying out loud. What kind of parent treats their kid like that?'

'We don't know for certain that you were ever shut in the cupboard.'

'No? It would explain why I feel spooked every time I walk near it. And why I suffer from severe claustrophobia. Oh, to hell with it all. I think maybe it's time to put the past behind me and move on. Let's just enjoy Christmas in this pretty village, and forget all about what might have happened forty years ago. Life's too short for this kind of navel-gazing nonsense.'

Karen squeezed his shoulder. 'If you're really sure, we'll let it go. I'm going to open that bottle of Dow's vintage port I brought along. A couple of glasses of that will make everything right.'

'Good idea,' Craig said, walking through to the kitchen for some glasses.

Karen was pouring the drinks when there was a sharp knock at the front door. She put down the bottle and opened the door. It was Michael Scrivener.

'Could I speak to you for a moment?' he said, not making full eye-contact with her. 'I've been thinking about that little chat we had this morning and there are a couple of things I didn't tell you.'

Karen shot an apprehensive glance at Craig, but he had no such misgivings. 'Come on in,' he said. 'We were just about to have a nip of Christmas port. I'll get another glass. Here, sit down on the settee.'

Karen took his overcoat and they made themselves comfortable around a low coffee table with their drinks in front of them. 'It's difficult to know where to start,' Scrivener said.

'A drink will loosen your tongue,' Karen said. 'Tell me, have you always run the butcher's shop in Great Somerford?'

Scrivener took a sip of port. 'Yes I have,' he said. 'It's the only job I've ever had.'

'So was it your ambition to be a butcher?' Karen asked.

He gave a nervous laugh. 'Not at all. As a matter of fact, I'd always been interested in electrical goods, you know, radios and televisions and the like. My ambition was to have my own TV shop, the idea being that apart from selling them, I could carry out my own repairs. I did a university course on business management and, as I'd been fortunate to inherit enough money to buy a shop, I started looking around for suitable premises. I saw in the local paper that the butcher's shop in Great Somerford was for sale and came here to look at it. I could see immediately that a TV shop in a village like this would have limited business scope, but I fell totally in love with the place. So I decided to buy the shop and keep it as a butcher's. Amazingly, I found I had a talent for selling meat, and I've never looked back.'

Craig grinned. 'It seems the drink has certainly loosened your tongue.'

'Don't be so rude,' Karen said.

'No, Craig is right,' Scrivener said, running his hand across his bald head. 'I came here to fill in some gaps I left earlier. I just need to decide where to start.'

Craig decided to jump straight in. 'Somebody mentioned you might have an old photo of my mum in your wallet. You could start by showing us that.'

Scrivener gave an embarrassed smile and reached into the inside pocket of his jacket. He opened his wallet and took out a well-worn black-and-white snap. 'I should have shown you this when you called round this morning,' he said, handing the photo over to Craig. 'Your mother was a very attractive girl.'

Craig stared hard at the picture. It was a head-and-shoulders photo, quite sharp despite its age. 'It's difficult to be objective about my own mother,' he said, 'but she does look pretty.' His hand was shaking as he handed the picture to Karen.

'She was an absolute stunner,' she said, turning to Michael Scrivener. 'You were hopelessly in love with her, weren't you?'

'Am I that transparent? Well, there's no point in denying it, not after all this time. Yes, I did love her. And I never have stopped loving her, actually. I'd have done anything for Rachael, anything at all. If she'd asked.' He slowly shook his head. 'Rachael Williams. The sound of her name sends a shiver through me, even to this day.'

'You had an affair with her?' Karen said. 'Behind Ian Rushton's back?'

'I wanted to, I'll not deny it. But Rachael wasn't the kind of girl to cheat.'

'Did she know how you felt about her?' Craig asked.

Scrivener grinned. 'Of course she did. I told her often enough. At the risk of sounding conceited, I'm certain she loved me too.' His expression hardened. 'If only she'd lived, things would have turned out so differently. She'd have ditched Ian Rushton, and moved in with me.'

'So you knew her well?' Craig said. 'You knew her much better than you let on to us this morning.'

'I'm sorry I was so guarded with you. I've never spoken to anybody about my relationship with Rachael and I find it hard to talk openly about it now.' He turned to Craig. 'But you are her son

93

and you deserve to know the truth about what happened.'

'The truth?' Craig picked up the old copy of the *Gazette and Herald* from the table. 'So the report in here doesn't give us the full story?'

Michael Scrivener shook his head. 'That inquest was a whitewash from start to finish. The fact is, your mother and Ian Rushton weren't getting on. He was a bully. She wanted to leave him, but was afraid.'

'Afraid?' Karen repeated. 'Afraid of what he might do?'

'He could be a nasty piece of work. He'd hit her before, on two occasions to my knowledge. He was a very jealous man.'

'And when my mother visited you in the evenings, no doubt he became even more jealous?'

'Absolutely. In the end I asked Rachael not to come, because I didn't want to risk her getting a beating.'

Craig clenched his fist. 'The bastard,' he said.

'On the day she died, she came to see me during the afternoon. She had told Rushton she was going to leave him. He had punched her hard in the stomach and forbidden her to go out, but she had somehow managed to struggle free of his clutches and had come straight round to see me. She was proud of herself for having summoned up the courage to tell him she was leaving him, but she was clearly in a good deal of pain. I was horrified and wanted her to see a doctor but she flatly refused. She stayed with me for several hours. We drank tea and chatted and eventually she started to feel better. I told her she was welcome to come and stay with me, and to bring her little boy – that's you of course, Craig – with her. I didn't want her to go back to Rushton at all, but she needed to collect a few essentials, and she was anxious about you, Craig, so I had to let her go. She promised she would return with you within the hour, but of course she never did. That was the last time I saw her alive.'

Craig frowned. 'But the newspaper account of the inquest makes no mention of her visit to you, or of the fact that she was leaving Rushton.'

'I didn't give evidence. I know this sounds bad, but I knew there would be no point. Ian Rushton told a very plausible story about Rachael storming out and getting drunk, and his version of events was accepted as the truth.'

'What about the local policeman who was called out to Holly Cottage? Surely he would have seen through Rushton?'

The policeman who attended the scene was Terry Smith, a lad in his twenties. He and Ian Rushton were best mates. Or perhaps more appropriately, as thick as thieves. Terry Smith was a bent cop who was later drummed out of the force, but at the time nobody knew that. He presented his version of events in such a way that he made Rushton seem like some kind of a saint. And poor Rachael was portrayed as a drunk who neglected her child.'

Karen jabbed a finger towards Michael Scrivener. 'Then why on earth didn't you stand up and tell the court that Rachael was with you that afternoon? And let everyone know that Rushton had hit her?'

Scrivener lowered his head. 'I know how it looks. In point of fact, I did pay a visit to Ian Rushton before the inquest, and I told him that Rachael had been with me and that I knew he'd punched her. I told him that I intended going to the police with the information I had. He flatly denied hitting her, and said that the doctor who had examined her body had confirmed that her injuries were entirely consistent with a fall down the stairs.

'He went on to say that if I told the court she had been with me that afternoon, he would provide male witnesses to swear that they had slept with her for money on numerous occasions. Rachael's name would have been completely destroyed.'

'My God, what an evil bastard,' Karen said. 'Do you think he would have actually done that?'

'I'm sure he would. Anyway, a couple of nights later while I was walking home from the pub, three guys waylaid me and gave me a hell of a beating. They broke my nose and three ribs. I didn't see their faces, but I have absolutely no doubt who had sent them.'

'Rushton was a nasty piece of work,' Craig said. 'I assume the police had no joy in identifying the thugs?'

'Not a chance. Professional lowlife. They took what little cash I had on me to make it look like theft, but it was all done to scare me off.' Scrivener pulled a hankie from his pocket and blew his nose. 'I'm ashamed to admit they succeeded.'

'You had no choice,' Craig said. 'You couldn't risk dragging my Mum's name through the mud. And it's not as if you could have brought her back.'

'It's just so unfair that Rushton was portrayed as a hero.' Karen said, turning to Craig. 'He got away with beating up your Mum.'

'I know,' Craig said. 'And we still can't be certain how she came to fall down the stairs.'

Michael Scrivener nodded. 'That has always been my greatest concern. We will never know the full details of how Rachael died, but the circumstances give rise to speculation. First and foremost, she was in a volatile relationship with a man who was known to be violent. On the day in question, she told him she was leaving him, and he had punched her in the stomach. She had somehow got away from him and disobeyed his orders by coming to see me. She did not return to him for several hours. It's safe to speculate that he would not have been in a pleasant frame of mind.

'The story given to the inquest was that Rachael was drunk when she returned to Holly Cottage, but that was completely untrue. I had given her one gin and tonic during the afternoon to help with the pain after being punched, but all we drank after that was tea. She was in a perfectly sober state when she left me, and there is no good reason why she would have fallen down the stairs after she arrived home. A far more plausible scenario is that Rachael and Ian Rushton argued and he pushed her. Of course we can't know that for certain. If only there had been a witness.'

'I agree,' Karen said. 'Although actually, there was a witness. A three-year-old boy.'

Craig forced a smile. 'I'm afraid my memory isn't as good as all that. I may have been there but I have no recollection of it whatsoever.'

'You were the sole reason Rachael was impatient to get back to Holly Cottage that afternoon,' Michael Scrivener said. 'She didn't trust Ian Rushton to be alone with you. He was mad at her and she was afraid he might vent his anger on you, Craig.'

'Christ! What the hell did she think he might have done to me?'

'Rachael told me they had an old-fashioned wardrobe in their bedroom. Evidently he used to lock you inside it when he felt especially vindictive. She told me it used to really upset you.'

Craig and Karen turned towards each other, and Karen put her arm around his shoulder. 'That explains a lot,' she said. 'Craig suffers from severe claustrophobia. We've been wondering if he was ever shut in the cupboard here, the one at the bottom of the stairs, but we obviously got that a bit wrong. It was a wardrobe, not the cupboard under the stairs.'

Craig tugged his ear. 'It also explains why I expected there to be a step up into that cupboard, when in fact there wasn't.'

Karen smiled. 'Of course. You were remembering having to step up into the wardrobe, each time you were shut in there.'

'At least we've cleared up that mystery,' Michael Scrivener said. 'I'm sorry I wasn't more frank with you when you called on me this morning.' He allowed himself an indulgent smile. 'I actually feel better now, having talked about it after all these years.'

'Me too,' Craig said. 'It's great to know that my mother wasn't an alcoholic, and fantastic to know that she wasn't the one who locked me in the wardrobe.'

'Your mother loved you,' Michael Scrivener said. 'She was a wonderful person, and you can be very proud of her.

After another glass of port each, they agreed to meet up that evening at the Volunteer Inn. Craig and Karen waved Michael Scrivener off as he started his short walk along the snow-covered High Street towards his butcher's shop. There was a chill in the late-afternoon air and they were glad to close the door and make themselves comfortable around the wood-burner.

'Feeling happier about things now?' Karen asked, curling up next to Craig on the settee.

'Definitely. Isn't it funny how you can get things so wrong? I was convinced my mum had neglected me, maybe even bullied me, and now, thanks to what Michael Scrivener told us, I can look back and think of her in a totally different light.'

'So do you think we're ready to go forward?'

He kissed her softly on the lips. 'Absolutely. If you feel the same.'

'It will mean I have to stop drinking alcohol.'

'Do you mind?' he asked.

'Of course not. Let's go for it.'

The Volunteer was busy that evening. Craig thanked Doug and Old Jim for their help, and treated them both to drinks. Michael Scrivener arrived shortly afterwards, and Karen and Craig found a table where the three of them could sit with some degree of privacy.

Michael raised his glass to them. 'I hope you enjoy your Christmas all the more now you know the full story about Rachael,' he said.

'Thanks for being so open about it,' Craig said, adding with a grin, 'in the end.'

'There's nothing else you want to tell us?' Karen said.

'There's nothing more to tell,' he said, scratching his ear.

Karen took a sip of her tonic water. 'You sure about that?'

Craig frowned. 'What's this all about?' he asked.

Karen looked Michael straight in the eyes. 'Remind us what became of that rat Ian Rushton,' she said.

Michael looked uncomfortable. 'He died a few months after Rachael,' he said. 'Rode his motorbike into a ditch and ended up with his head under water, unable to move.'

'Served him right,' Craig said.

'Oh, yes,' Michael added.

'It was the only way you could get justice for the girl you loved, wasn't it?' Karen said.

Michael took a long drink from his glass. 'I've kept quiet for nearly forty years. If you think I'm going to confess now, you're going to be disappointed.'

'I don't want your confession,' Karen said. 'I just needed to know.'

Craig stood up and patted him on the back. 'And I'd like to buy you another drink.'

'Before you do that,' Karen said, 'I think Michael has something else to tell you. That's right, isn't it?'

Michael Scrivener put down his glass and lowered his head. He was shaking.

'Would somebody like to tell me what the hell is going on?' Craig asked.

Michael looked up again, tears streaming down his face. 'I've wanted to tell you ever since you came to my house yesterday morning. I wanted to scream it from the rooftops. But I didn't have the guts. I daren't risk being rejected.' He turned to Karen. 'How did you know?'

She smiled. 'A few tell-tale signs, like you both having the same twinkling blue eyes, and the way you both pull on your earlobe when you're stressed. But the fact that both you and Rachael went to university at around the time Craig was conceived…well, it's not rocket science, is it?'

Craig looked shocked. 'Are you saying that Michael…'

Karen stood up and squeezed his shoulder. 'Say hello to your Dad, Craig.'

The three of them hugged, the two men crying like babies.

'This has to be the best Christmas lunch of my entire life,' Craig said.

'Are you referring to the company, or my cooking?' Karen asked.

'Both. A proper family Christmas, in the company of my lovely wife, and my new-found Dad.'

Michael Scrivener rose to his feet. 'I'd like to drink to the health of my son, and his beautiful wife.' He turned to Craig. 'I had no way of tracing your whereabouts and I thought I'd never see you again. This is the best Christmas present I could ever have wished for. I'd like to propose a toast to the two of you.'

They raised their glasses. Karen was drinking water.

'No alcohol for you?' Michael asked. 'Any reason?'

'Let's hope there is,' she said. 'That would round off everything perfectly.'

MOVING ON

Lucy picked up the post from the doormat and carried it through to the kitchen. Three Christmas cards, she could tell that without opening them. She recognised the handwriting on the first two envelopes and tossed them onto the table. The third one though was more intriguing; she was certain she had never seen that handwriting before.

It was a cute card; a snowman kissing a snow-girl under a sprig of mistletoe. The message inside was in the same unfamiliar handwriting as the envelope.

'Go on, make my Christmas; meet me at the bar in Gluggers *on Christmas Eve at eight o'clock. I'll wear a sprig of holly in my buttonhole so you'll know it's me.'*

This just had to be from Alexander, Lucy told herself. He's got a nerve. Even so, she walked out to the car with a spring in her step.

Barry's Baguettes was a thriving bakery and sandwich bar in the town centre. Lucy's father had been running it for the past ten years and had transformed it from a modest affair into a highly successful business. Lucy had joined as his Accounts Manager after leaving college two years ago. She really enjoyed the job, and the pay meant she could afford her own flat and car.

At coffee break, she showed the Christmas card to Natasha, her workmate and best friend. 'Do you think Alexander might have sent this?'

Natasha considered the matter as she took a bite from her chocolate éclair. 'I wouldn't think so. You split up almost six months ago. Surely you're not still hankering after him?'

'We were together for a year.'

'He was a two-timing snake, Lucy. You deserve better.'

'Like who, for example?'

Natasha didn't give a direct reply. She licked a blob of cream from her perfectly manicured fingernail. 'The handwriting on this card looks awkward; it's obviously been disguised. Someone from work is my guess. What about Matt?'

'I wish,' said Lucy. 'He never even looks at me.'

'Why don't you make the first move?'

'I've lost confidence in myself since Alexander. Besides, I don't believe Matt sent the card.'

'If you say so. Listen, I've had another idea. Perhaps Crawley sent it.'

'Not Creepy Crawley, please.'

'Good morning, girls,' said an unwelcome intruder.

'Hello, Crawley,' Natasha said. 'We were just talking about you.'

He smoothed his hand over his hair. 'I suppose you were arguing about which of you lucky babes is taking me out tonight.'

'How did you guess?'

'Let's make it a threesome.'

'We're having a private conversation if you don't mind,' Lucy said.

He blew her a kiss and made a hasty retreat.

Lucy's dad was in the office when she returned after lunch. His rosy cheeks and warm smile made her think of Santa Claus, and she tried hard to look happy. There was no fooling him though.

'About time you got Alexander out of your system, isn't it?' he said. 'He was never right for you.'

She started to protest but changed her mind. 'You're right, Dad. It's time I moved on.'

He put his arm around her shoulder. 'That's my girl. Time to stop moping and have some fun. Christmas is almost here.'

'It'll be strange spending Christmas Day on my own in the flat.'

'Your Mum and I would be thrilled if you spent the day back at home with us.'

'Thanks. I might take you up on that.'

'Lovely.'

She had another chat with Natasha before going home that evening. 'Any more thoughts on my mysterious Christmas card?' she said.

'My money's on Matt,' Natasha said. 'Talk of the devil...'

The door opened and Matt entered wearing his white overalls and baker's hat. He walked straight past Lucy, and spoke to Natasha. 'Phew, it's hot in the baking room.'

'All set for Christmas?' she asked.

'Is it that time of year already?'

'Surely you've sent your Christmas cards? It's the last day of posting tomorrow.'

'I haven't sent any cards yet. Haven't even bought any. Might pop into the market in the morning.'

'Very trendy.'

'Must get on. See you.'

As soon as he'd gone, Lucy turned to Natasha. 'We can rule *him* out. He hasn't sent *any* cards.'

'He may have been bluffing.'

'He sounded genuine to me. And let's face it, he didn't even glance in my direction.'

'A sure sign he fancies you.'

'No such luck.'

It was Christmas Eve.

'I take it you haven't discovered who sent that cryptic Christmas card,' Natasha said, munching a mince pie.

'No,' Lucy said. 'And I certainly won't bother turning up at *Gluggers*. If a boy wants to take me out, he can ask me to my face.'

Crawley wandered over to them. Natasha nudged him. 'Doing anything special tonight?' she asked.

He leered at her. 'Is that an offer?'

'I'm not that desperate. Anyway, I heard you were meeting someone at *Gluggers*.'

'Might be. Depends.'

'On what?'

He tapped the side of his nose and strolled off. Matt walked in. Lucy looked up to wish him a happy Christmas, but he turned away before she could speak.

'Get stuffed, then,' she murmured.

She left work at half-past four. She didn't feel in the mood for Christmas. Someone was waiting for her outside the office; someone she hadn't seen for months.

Alexander.

'Can I walk you home?' he asked uneasily.

She nodded. He looked older, or perhaps not so well.

'I was hoping to catch you,' he said. 'I've been thinking about you a lot.'

'Really?'

'Look, about me and…that's all over. It meant nothing. I've never stopped loving you.'

'Do you want to pick up where we left off?'

He turned to face her, placing his hand on her shoulder. 'Yes, I want that more than anything.'

Lucy pulled sharply away from him. 'After the way you hurt me? Seeing somebody else behind my back, unceremoniously dumping me. You broke my bloody heart. It's over, Alexander. Goodbye.'

She walked on, leaving him dumbstruck. She felt good. A weight had been lifted from her. And she knew now, at last, she really could move on.

She propped the Christmas card in front of her as she tucked into her evening meal, reading the message once more, and scrutinising the writing. She was convinced now that it wasn't Alexander's writing. So who the hell had sent it? It would be fun to find out. And suddenly it didn't even matter if it was Crawley.

Time to get made up, she told herself. She hadn't been to *Gluggers* for ages.

The place was packed. She was waiting to get served at the bar when she found herself face to face with someone she knew. To her disappointment she saw that it was indeed Crawley.

'Hi, gorgeous, fancy meeting you here,' he said.

She had committed herself to go through with this. 'Just fancy.'

'It seems everyone's in here tonight.' He pointed to the middle distance. 'I saw Matt back there. He looked ridiculous, wearing a great big sprig of holly.'

Lucy had already headed off in that direction. 'You!' she said.

'You!' replied Matt from behind the holly. He looked genuinely shocked.

Lucy produced the Christmas card from her bag. 'You sent this, asking me to meet you here tonight?'

He gave her an odd look as he fished in his pocket. 'Snap,' he said, placing an identical card next to hers. 'I was instructed to come here wearing a sprig of holly.'

'I don't understand…?' she began.

'We've been set up. Someone sent us both a card to push us together.'

'Push us together?' She couldn't disguise her disappointment. 'I knew you didn't fancy me.'

'Of course I fancy you,' he said. 'I really fancy you.'

'You've got a funny way of showing it. You never even look at me.'

'I've forced myself not to get involved. I just daren't risk losing my job.'

'What the hell are you talking about?'

'I'd better explain,' he said. 'I lost my last job because I started dating the boss's daughter. He sacked me on the spot when he found out. It took ages to find this job, and I really enjoy it. So you see…'

'But my dad isn't like that.'

'To be honest, I'm not worried any more. I can see now I've been a fool. You're worth far more to me than any job. If your father…'

'My dad won't object.'

A rosy-cheeked man interrupted them. 'Did I hear my name mentioned?'

'Dad! What on earth are you doing here? You're far too old for a place like this!'

'Whoops,' said Matt.

116

'I had to look in, just to see if you both turned up.'

'It was *you!*' Lucy shrieked. '*You* sent those cards! How dare you meddle in my affairs?'

'Well, you've been looking so miserable lately. And it was perfectly obvious that Matt was keen on you, so I decided to help it along a bit. Now, do you want me to stay as a chaperone, just in case you two don't get on?'

Lucy felt Matt gently squeeze her hand. She hadn't felt so happy for ages. 'I don't think that's going to be necessary, Dad. Thanks all the same.'

Her dad grinned. He looked more like Santa than ever.

PERFECT MATCH

Nicola put down her spoon and shot an embarrassed glance around the restaurant. She'd already had more wine than was good for her, but Brandon was insisting he refill her glass. It wasn't as if he was being pleasant about it.

'Don't be such a spoilsport,' he slurred, carelessly spilling wine on the tablecloth. 'And try smiling for a change. You're only twenty! You look as miserable as those old fogies over there.'

The elderly couple at the next table pretended not to notice but it was hard to ignore Brandon when he'd had a drink. He stood up and announced he was going to the toilet, clumsily knocking the table and tipping over the lighted candle. Nicola made a grab for it, but luckily it had gone out.

He'd been a pain all evening. It had been a mistake to come to a decent restaurant, particularly one specialising in up-market Turkish cuisine; Brandon would have been more at home at a burger bar. As he disappeared into the toilet, the immaculately-dressed waiter glided over with a silver tray balanced on the tips of his fingers.

'Perhaps Madam would prefer something non-alcoholic?' he said, exchanging her glass for the one on his tray. 'I think sparkling apple juice would suit you better.'

Nicola smiled. 'Thank you so much. I simply couldn't face any more wine.'

'Your partner, he does not understand such things,' the waiter said, straightening the candle in the centre of the table. He produced a book of matches and struck one with a flourish, touching the flame against the wick. The table was bathed in a warm orange glow. 'The candlelight gives your complexion a radiance,' he said. 'Beautiful.'

It was twaddle of course, but Nicola was grateful all the same. Brandon didn't do compliments. The waiter bowed to Nicola and ceremoniously handed her the book of matches.

'A souvenir of your night at our humble Turkish restaurant,' he said, making a swift exit seconds before Brandon arrived back at the table.

Nicola had always loved Christmas. Coloured lights, crisp winter weather, decorations and cards. Carols. Crackers. The smell of pine. She missed that. Nicola hadn't had a real Christmas tree for three years now, not since she'd moved in with Brandon.

She fished through the box of decorations and lifted out a pretty Father Christmas made of red and green glass. It hadn't taken long to realise that Brandon was not a Christmas person. The first couple of years he'd allowed her to put up a few trimmings, but last year he'd been so unpleasant that Nicola hadn't bothered. She tried not to feel sorry for herself. Some people were far worse off than she was. Her friend Fran, for instance. Her young son Dexter was in hospital with a serious heart problem and she was anxiously waiting for the test results. It put things into perspective.

Nicola peered through the window at the snow-filled sky, dull and overcast. She looked again at the glass Father Christmas. She'd bought it from *Ikea* a few years back. You lit a candle at the back to illuminate it. She cast her mind back to the night before at the Turkish restaurant and reflected how much she'd enjoyed the candlelight. Why not light the Father Christmas candle now? She knew exactly where to lay her hands on a book of matches.

She hadn't noticed at the time how pretty the cover was, brightly coloured with oriental-style lettering. *Jeannie's Turkish Diner.* The waiter had presented it to her as though it was worth the world, yet there were just three matches left. Still, it had been a kind gesture.

She tore out one of the matches, struck it, and lit the candle. The dreariness of the room was transformed into a colourful glow. Nicola gazed around, mesmerised. There was something magical about the flickering shadows on the wall and ceiling. Unfortunately, the spell was broken when she noticed the unscrubbed potatoes and carrots on the worktop

'I *really* wish I didn't have to cook a meal tonight,' she said with feeling.

The telephone rang.

'Hi Nicola, it's Fran here. This is extremely short notice, but I'm having a party tonight, what with Christmas only a week away. And it'll help take my mind off things.'

'Have you had any news from the hospital?'

'Still waiting for the test results. The doctor didn't sound too optimistic.'

'You poor thing. And poor little Dexter. Is there anything I can do?'

'Yes, come and support me at the party tonight. You can bring Brandon too, even though I think you should dump him. Where is he, football?'

'How did you guess? It's the only thing he gets excited about these days.'

'Oh dear, it sounds like a night out will do you good. You will come, won't you?'

'Will there be food?'

'Well, really!'

Sorry, Fran, I didn't mean it to sound like that. To be honest, I don't feel like cooking tonight.'

'Come along to my party and you won't have to. You will come?'

'I'd love to. See you later.' Nicola hung up, smiling to herself. She felt brighter now. She'd have a bath and make herself up.

It didn't dawn on her until she was soaking in the soapy water.

She'd made a wish that she wouldn't have to cook a meal tonight and, *hey presto*, suddenly she didn't have to. It was after she'd struck that match. What if they were magic matches? Strike a match and make a wish. Jeannie's Turkish Diner matches. It was like Genie and the lamp where you rubbed the lamp and were granted three wishes. Of course, it was a ridiculous notion. But she had two matches left. There was no harm in trying.

Brandon came home while she was putting on her make-up, and the idea went out of her head. United had gone down four-nil at home. She heard him swearing as he took a bottle of lager from the fridge. He put his head round the bedroom door and belched.

'Where's dinner? I'm starving.'

'I'm not cooking,' Nicola said. 'Fran's invited us to her Christmas party.'

'That's why you're tarting yourself up like a Christmas tree, is it?' His eyes moved to her black dress. 'You needn't think you're wearing that. Showing off your body to everyone. Put some jeans on.'

'It's a party. Besides, I thought you liked this dress.'

'That doesn't mean I want anyone else seeing you in it.'

'So it's for your eyes only?'

'What's this all about? You're *my* woman, remember? I don't want to go out tonight anyway. There's football on the telly later.' He stormed back into the kitchen.

Things had changed during the three years they'd lived together. At first Nicola had been happy, full of fun and sparkle. Bur gradually Brandon had burst all the bubbles, and her self-confidence had gone down the plughole along with the bathwater. Now she was frightened to stand up to him, frightened to leave him. When he was angry he would catch hold of her so tightly she would bruise.

She changed into a more modest floral dress, and agreed they'd be home by ten.

At least Brandon was enjoying the party. He'd spent the past hour peering down the front of the dress of the blonde divorcee from number 19. She was on the lookout for husband number five. Her previous partners had wound up either bankrupt or deceased. The last one had been bankrupt *and* deceased.

Nicola was past caring about his flirting, but she felt uncomfortable on her own. She glanced over at Fran and forced a smile. This was embarrassing. She looked down and noticed the book-match in her handbag. Of course! The three wishes.

She struck the second match and watched as it burst into life with a huge flame. As the flame died down, she looked skywards and clenched her fists.

'I wish,' she said, concentrating. 'I wish to swap my so-called boyfriend. I'd like a new man, please. Someone kind and caring, someone who won't hurt me.'

As if at some pre-arranged signal, Brandon left the room with the blonde. Nicola scanned the room for her new man. Disappointed, she made her way over to the buffet table. As she stood there surveying the spread, she heard a soft, masculine voice behind her.

'Try the sausage rolls,' it said. 'They're good. I made them.'

She turned around eagerly and found herself staring into a pair of deep brown eyes. Then she took in the rest of the man's appearance; short, almost bald, overweight, and probably in his sixties. The second button of his cardigan was fastened through the third buttonhole.

'I'm Ted,' he said slowly. 'Ted Newman.'

'Ted...ahh...new man. I see. Do excuse me a moment, there's something I have to sort out.' Nicola retreated into a corner and stared up at the ceiling. 'Very funny!' she whispered to no one in particular. 'You know what I meant by a new man. Couldn't you find someone nearer my age? And while you're about it, couldn't he be reasonably good-looking? Please don't think I'm being fussy. It's not like I'm asking him to look like one of the boys in One Direction.'

'Excuse me, did you say something?'

She spun round in surprise. The young man in front of her seemed to have sprung from nowhere. He was, without doubt, absolutely gorgeous, and with his luxurious mop of dark brown hair he bore a remarkable resemblance to Harry Styles. Nicola tried to speak but her voice had dried up. The newcomer continued. 'I'm sorry, I haven't introduced myself. I'm Christopher. I've just moved into the house across the road. Are you here on your own?'

Nicola glanced around the room. 'Yes,' she squeaked.

'Can I get you a drink?'

'Please. A white wine spritzer.'

Christopher smiled. 'Your wish is my command. I've a feeling you and me are gonna hit it off fine.' He went over to get the drink.

Nicola sighed. 'So do I, Harry, so do I.'

Ted Newman wandered over. 'My lighter's packed up. You don't mind if I borrow a match to light my pipe?' He tore out the last match from her book, and struck it. The familiar orange glow filled the room. The old boy puffed on his pipe.

Nicola couldn't contain her anger. 'How dare you,' she screeched. 'That was a special match.'

'I must say it did burn with a hell of a flame.'

'It was my last one.'

'Oh dear, I'm sorry to have upset you like this. I wish I hadn't used it now.'

'You *wish* you hadn't used it?' Nicola's expression brightened. She took the match-book from him and opened it.

'That's odd,' Ted said, 'there's one left. I could have sworn I'd used the last one.' He smiled. 'All's well that ends well.'

The following night, Christopher called round to help Nicola decorate her Christmas tree. A real one of course. While he was there, Fran arrived. She was so happy she could hardly get the words out.

Little Dexter had made a miraculous recovery and had been discharged from hospital. 'Oh, Nicola,' she said, 'I couldn't have wished for anything better.'

Nicola glanced at the waste bin where she'd thrown her empty matchbook.

'Neither could I,' she said.

- *Winner of Warminster Writers' Circle Winter competition*
- *Shortlisted for* Bath Chronicle *Winter's Tale short story competition*
- *Joint winner of Frome Prose Café Christmas competition*
- *Published in* Take a Break *magazine*

Lightning Source UK Ltd.
Milton Keynes UK
UKOW02f0157310814

237805UK00001B/17/P